The Hunt for the Yeti Skull: NEPAL

Join Secret Agent Jack Stalwart

on his other adventures:

The Search for the Sunken Treasure: **AUSTRALIA**

The Secret of the Sacred Temple: **CAMBODIA**

The Escape of the Deadly Dinosaur: **USA**

The Puzzle of the Missing Panda: **CHINA**

The Mystery of the Mona Lisa: **FRANCE**

The Caper of the Crown Jewels: **ENGLAND**

Peril at the Grand Prix: **ITALY**

The Pursuit of the Ivory Poachers: **KENYA**

The Deadly Race to Space: **RUSSIA**

The Quest for Aztec Gold: **MEXICO**

The Theft of the Samurai Sword: **JAPAN**

The Fight for the Frozen Land: **ARCTIC**

The Hunt for the Yeti Skull: NEPAL

Elizabeth Singer Hunt

Illustrated by Brian Williamson

WEINSTEIN BOOKS

Originally published in Great Britain under the same title in slightly different form

 Printed in the United States of America. For information address Weinstein Books, 387 Park Avenue South, 12th Floor, New York, NY 10016.

ISBN: 978-1-60286-151-0
E-Book ISBN: 978-1-60286-155-8

First Edition

LSC-C

10 9 8 7 6 5

To Andy, my stalwart companion

THE WORLD

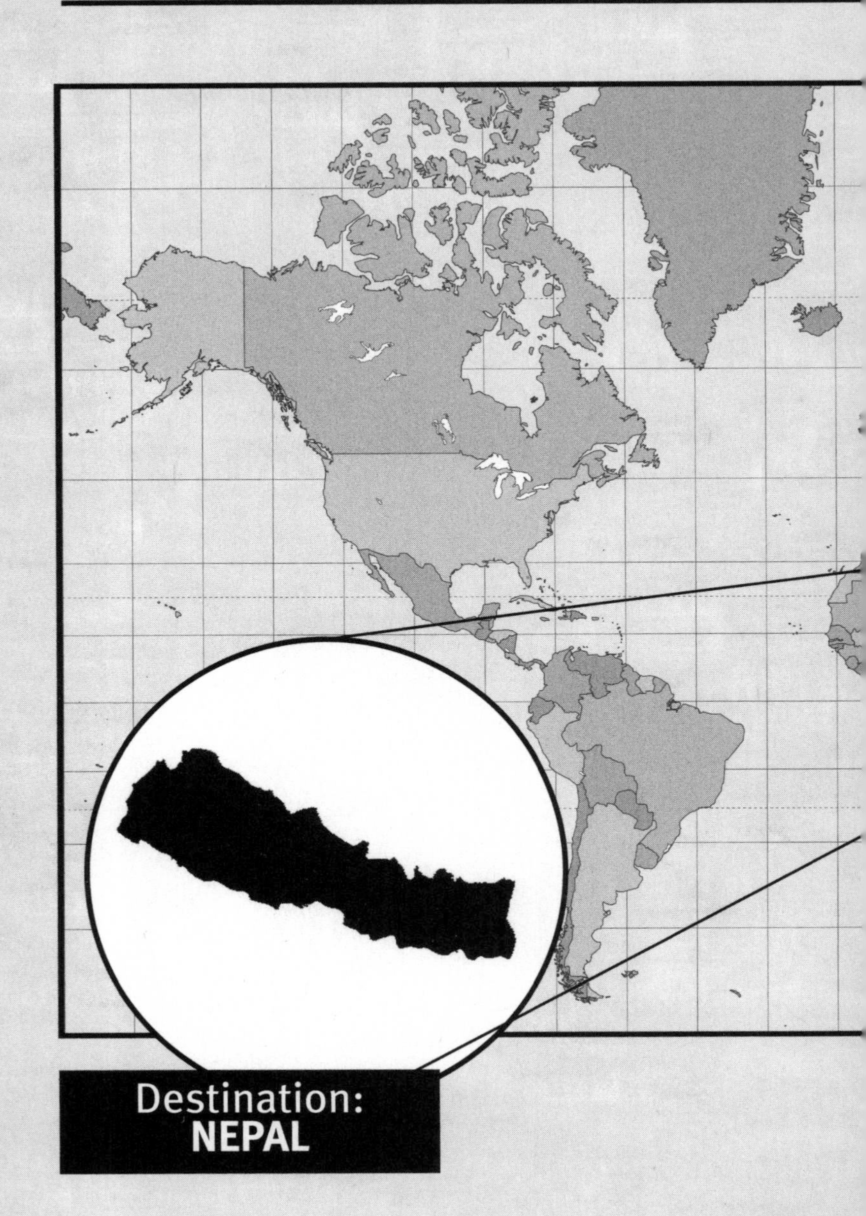

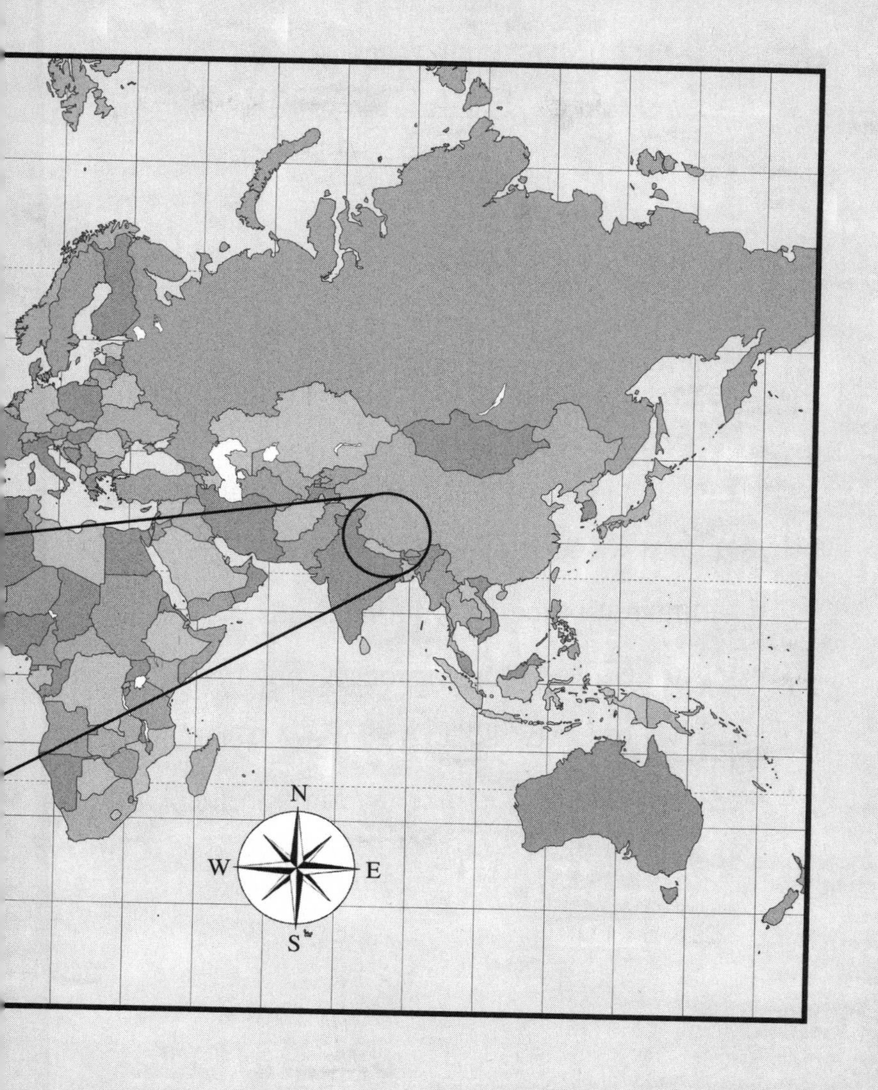
N
W
E
S

GLOBAL PROTECTION FORCE FILE ON

JACK STALWART

Jack Stalwart applied to be a secret agent for the Global Protection Force four months ago.

My name is Jack Stalwart. My older brother, Max, was a secret agent for you, until he disappeared on one of your missions. Now I want to be a secret agent too. If you choose me, I will be an excellent secret agent and get rid of evil villains, just like my brother did.

Sincerely,

Jack Stalwart

GLOBAL PROTECTION FORCE INTERNAL MEMO:
HIGHLY CONFIDENTIAL

Jack Stalwart was sworn in as a Global Protection Force secret agent four months ago. Since that time, he has completed all of his missions successfully and has stopped no less than thirteen evil villains. Because of this he has been assigned the code name 'COURAGE'.

Jack has yet to uncover the whereabouts of his brother, Max, who is still working for this organization at a secret location. Do not give Secret Agent Jack Stalwart this information. He is never to know about his brother.

Gerald Barter

Gerald Barter
Director, Global Protection Force

THINGS YOU'LL FIND IN EVERY BOOK

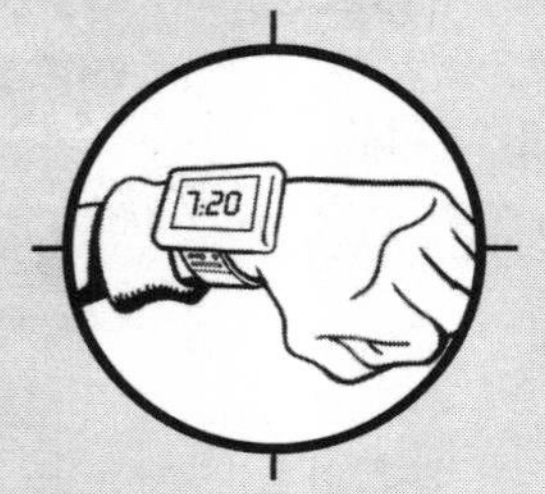

Watch Phone: The only gadget Jack wears all the time, even when he's not on official business. His Watch Phone is the central gadget that makes most others work. There are lots of important features, most importantly the 'C' button, which reveals the code of the day – necessary to unlock Jack's Secret Agent Book Bag. There are buttons on both sides, one of which ejects his life-saving Melting Ink Pen. Beyond these functions, it also works as a phone and, of course, gives Jack the time of day.

Global Protection Force (GPF): The GPF is the organization Jack works for. It's a worldwide force of young secret agents whose aim is to protect the world's people, places and possessions. No one knows exactly where its main offices are located (all correspondence and gadgets for repair are sent to a special PO Box, and training is held at various locations around the world), but Jack thinks it's somewhere cold, like the Arctic Circle.

Whizzy: Jack's magical miniature globe. Almost every night at precisely 7:30 p.m., the GPF uses Whizzy to send Jack the identity of the country that he must travel to. Whizzy can't talk, but he can cough up messages. Jack's parents don't know Whizzy is anything more than a normal globe.

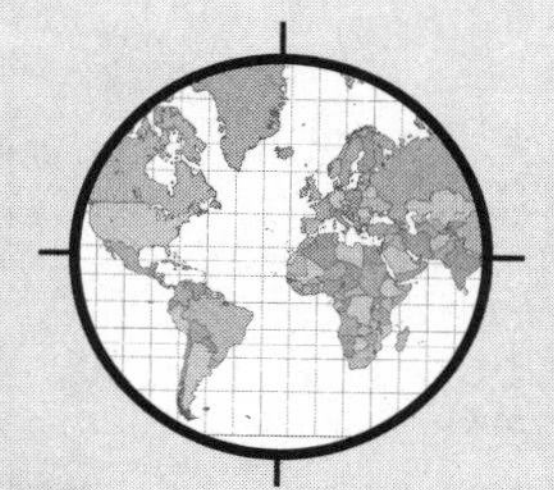

The Magic Map: The magical map hanging on Jack's bedroom wall. Unlike most maps, the GPF's map is made of a mysterious wood. Once Jack inserts the country piece from Whizzy, the map swallows Jack whole and sends him away on his missions. When he returns, he arrives precisely one minute after he left.

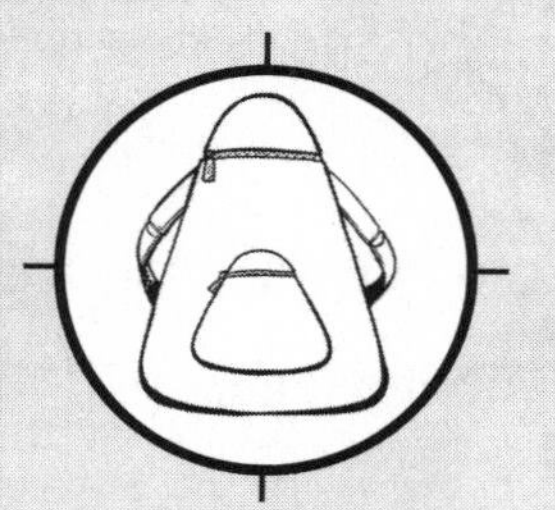

Secret Agent Book Bag: The Book Bag that Jack wears on every adventure. Licensed only to GPF secret agents, it contains top-secret gadgets necessary to foil bad guys and escape certain death. To activate the bag before each mission, Jack must punch in a secret code given to him by his Watch Phone. Once he's away, all he has to do is place his finger on the zip, which identifies him as the owner of the bag and immediately opens.

THE STALWART FAMILY

Jack's dad, John

He moved the family to England when Jack was two, in order to take a job with an aerospace company. Jack's dad thinks he is an ordinary boy and that his other son, Max, attends a school in Switzerland. Jack's dad is American and his mom is British, which makes Jack a bit of both.

Jack's mom, Corinne

One of the greatest moms as far as Jack is concerned. When she and her husband received a letter from a posh school in Switzerland inviting Max to attend, they were overjoyed. Since Max left six months ago, they have received numerous notes in Max's handwriting telling them he's OK. Little do they know it's all a lie and that it's the GPF sending those letters.

Jack's older brother, Max

Two years ago, at the age of nine, Max joined the GPF. Max used to tell Jack about his adventures and show him how to work his secret-agent gadgets. When the family received a letter inviting Max to attend a school in Europe, Jack figured it was to do with the GPF. Max told him he was right, but that he couldn't tell Jack anything about why he was going away.

Nine-year-old Jack Stalwart

Four months ago, Jack received an anonymous note saying: 'Your brother is in danger. Only you can save him.' As soon as he could, Jack applied to be a secret agent too. Since that time, he's battled some of the world's most dangerous villains, and hopes some day in his travels to find and rescue his brother, Max.

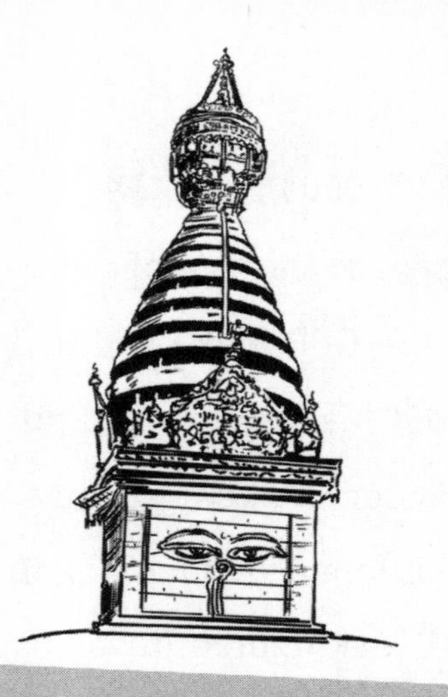

DESTINATION: *Nepal*

The country of Nepal lies between India and China, on the continent of Asia.

•

Its capital city is called Kathmandu (pronounced Kat-man-doo). People have lived in the Kathmandu Valley for at least 9,000 years.

•

The majority of Nepalese people are farmers. They grow tea, rice, corn, wheat and sugarcane.

There's an ancient Buddhist temple in the valley called the Monkey Temple, because holy monkeys live inside it. You have to climb 365 steps to get to it.

•

In the north of Nepal are the Himalayas, a mountain range. Eight of the world's tallest mountains (including Mount Everest, Kangchenjunga and Lhotse), are found in Nepal.

FOR NEPAL

Hello
namaste (pronounced nah-MAH-stay)

My name is...
mero naam … ho (pronounced MAY-ro-na-m…ho)

Thank you
dhanybhad (pronounced DHAN-naii-bat)

Have a nice day
subha din (pronounced sub-HA-din)

I'm from...
mero ghara ... ho (pronounced me-ro GHA-ra…ho)

Mount Everest: FACTS AND FIGURES

Mount Everest is the tallest mountain in the world, as measured from sea level. It stands at 29,029 feet tall.

The local people call it Mount Chomolungma. However, most of the world knows it by its English name, Everest. It was named after Sir George Everest, who used to be the Surveyor General of India in the 1800s.

On May 29th 1953, Sir Edmund Hillary and Sherpa Tenzing Norgay made history by being the first men to climb to the summit of Everest, and stand 'on top of the world'.

Mount Everest: FACTS AND FIGURES

ROUTE MAP

GPF: FAST FACTS

On May 22nd 2010 Jordan Romero, aged thirteen, became the youngest person to climb Everest.

Mount Everest is considered dangerous to climb because of its altitude (or height). The altitude can cause sickness in the brain and lungs.

Mountain climbers begin climbing Everest at either North Base Camp in Tibet or South Base Camp in Nepal, where they spend many days getting used to the altitude so they can avoid the sickness.

GPF Climbing Guide

There are lots of different types of climbing – make sure to take lessons with a proper teacher before you try them!

'Bouldering' is where you scramble over large rocks using your hands and feet, rather than ropes, and with a crash pad for safety. You can do this outside on natural rock, or at an indoor climbing place.

'Ice climbing' is scaling an ice wall using a harness, rope, ice axe and crampons. Crampons are spikes attached to the bottom of your boots that dig into the ice to stop you from slipping.

'Mountain climbing' can use the techniques above – people attempting to climb tall mountains must carry enough equipment, food and water with them, since it can take days to reach the top.

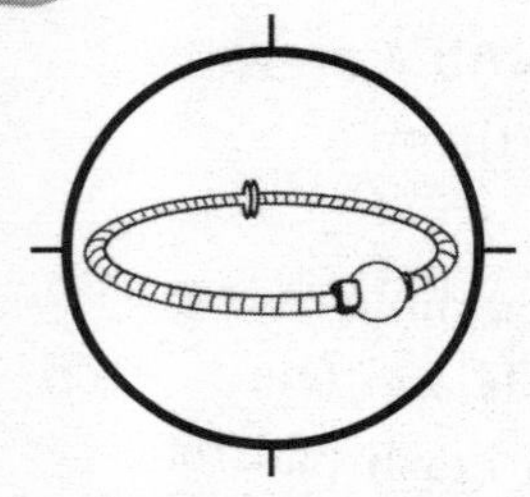

Oxygen Exchanger: If you're climbing mountains or diving underwater, strap on the GPF's Oxygen Exchanger. This two-part device converts the carbon dioxide that you breathe out into fresh oxygen whenever you need it. Comes with a wrap-around breathing tube and mouthpiece.

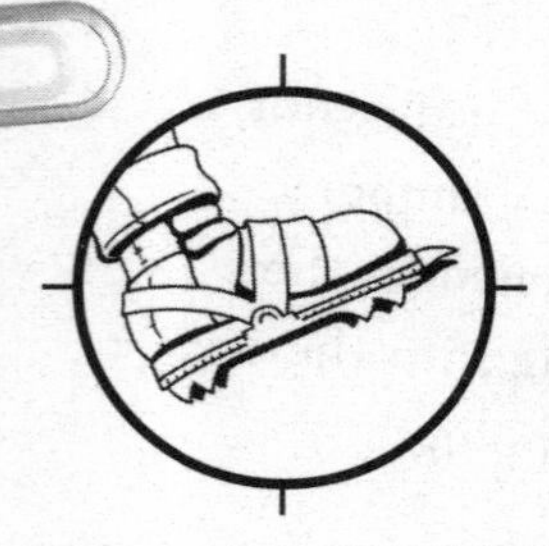

Crafty Crampons: The GPF's Crafty Crampons provide just enough 'stick' to prevent you from slipping on icy surfaces. Just strap these spiky, steel frames onto the bottom of your boots. The frames automatically adjust from flexible to rigid, depending on whether you're walking or ice climbing.

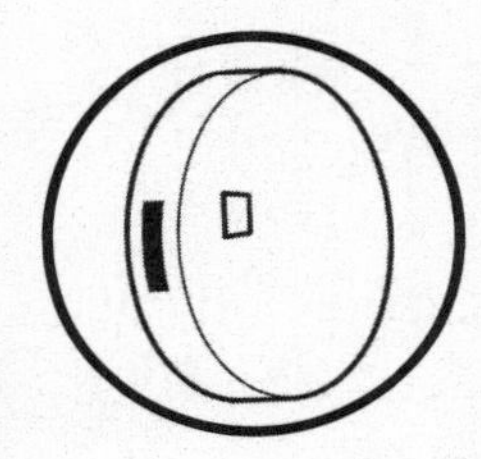

Klimbing Kit: When you need a powerful rope for climbing, use the GPF's Klimbing Kit. Just point the hatch of this circular case in the direction you want, and push the 'eject' button. Instantly, one of three ropes will fling out. If you need to fix the rope, tie a spike at the end before ejecting.

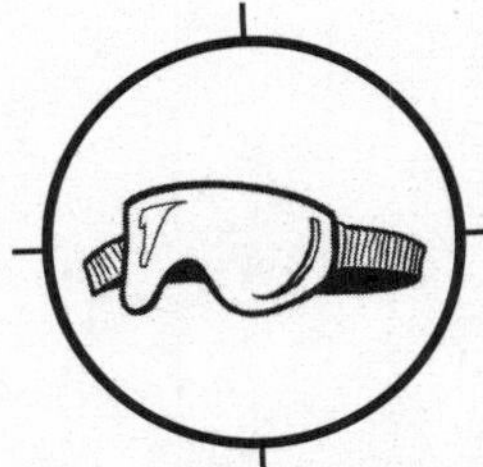

Snow Shades:
To prevent snow blindness in high altitudes, wear your GPF Snow Shades. Like the Google Goggles, the Snow Shades also have a built-in zoom feature that's activated by flicking a small switch on the side of the lens.

Chapter 1: The Indoor Wall

WUMPH!

Jack slapped his right hand onto the artificial rock face above him. He slid it to the right and wrapped his fingers around a plastic grip. Then he stretched his leg over onto a ledge and lifted his body upwards.

Suddenly he heard a high-pitched voice from his left: 'Beat you to the top, Stalwart!'

Jack turned to look. It was Marko

Mayer. Marko had recently arrived in England, having been adopted by a couple in Surrey. He was also one of the most annoying people Jack had ever met. The boys were in the same class at Planit Rockit, Surrey's biggest indoor rock-climbing facility. Whoever managed to ring the bell at the top of the wall first would win.

'I don't think so!' Jack shouted back.

Up to his left was another hand-hold. Jack reached out and grabbed onto it with all his strength. Heaving himself upwards, he quickly looked for another grip. Marko was already a full body's length ahead.

'Come on, Jack!' yelled a distant voice. It was Richard, one of Jack's best friends. Richard was Jack's 'belaying partner', or the person who controlled the safety of Jack's rope from below. 'You can do it!'

Jack was really sweating now. After

climbing for nearly ten minutes, his muscles were quivering. He glanced down, past the nylon rope dangling to his side. Everything and everyone looked far away. That's what happened when you were six storeys off the ground.

According to the Alti-Meter on his Watch Phone, Jack was sixty-five feet high, and he had another ten to go. Up to the left was another slim plastic grip. If Jack could reach it, he might get the break he needed.

Stretching his body across, Jack pressed his cheek to the rock face and felt down with his foot to find another ledge. He managed to pull himself over to it. From there, the holds were easier to reach and Jack was able to gain some speed. Now, he and Marko were racing neck and neck for the bell.

'Ring it!' shouted Richard.

But Marko was shimmying across the wall towards Jack. Instead of stepping on a ledge, he purposefully stepped on Jack's fingers.

CRUNCH.

Jack yelped in pain and immediately let go of the hand-hold. His body fell fast, and skidded several feet down the wall before Richard locked off the rope. Jack's body stopped with a severe jolt. He hung there in his harness, swaying back and forth.

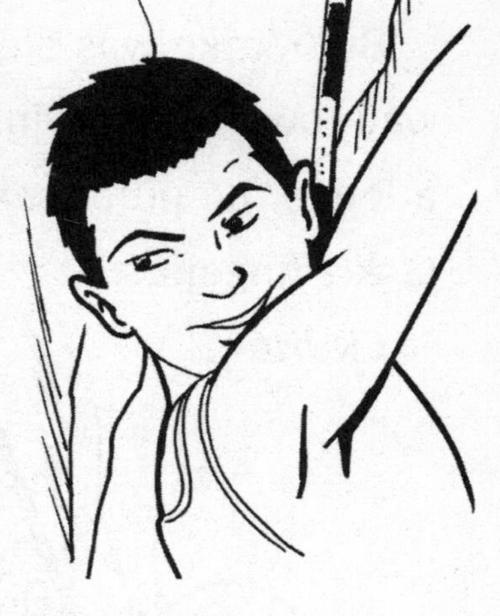

DING!

The bell rang from above. Marko raised his hand in triumph and gave a smug grin.

'Well done!' said a voice from below. It was Mr Matheson, their climbing coach. 'Why don't you boys come down?'

Jack abseiled to the ground, bouncing his feet off the wall. Instead of taking it slowly, Marko sailed to the floor as fast as he could.

'Told you I'd beat you,' he boasted as he passed Jack.

'Cheat!' yelled Jack.

As soon as Jack's feet touched the floor, Richard was at his side.

'What happened up there?' he asked.

Jack rolled his eyes as he took off his helmet and harness.

Coach Matheson walked over to Marko and slapped him on the back. 'Nice job,' he said, congratulating Marko. It was obvious that he hadn't seen the cheating going on. 'You're the champ of the day.'

Marko snickered.

Jack wanted to tell his coach what had really happened, but sometimes being a tattletale was worse than cheating. Besides, Jack figured, Marko would get what was coming to him sooner or later.

'Time's up,' said Coach Matheson. 'Pack up your gear. See you next week.'

Jack looked towards the glass exit doors. As always, his dad was waiting for him. Jack said goodbye to Richard and walked over to his father.

'Hi, Dad,' he said, his shoulders slumped.

Across the way, Marko was with his dad. The man was congratulating his adopted son.

'Don't let it bother you, pal,' his father said. 'After all, you're the best climber in the county. You have a trophy to prove it.'

'Thanks,' said Jack, trying to smile.

Jack's dad put his arm around his son and the two of them left the climbing center.

Chapter 2: Breaking News

As soon as Jack got home, he told his mom what had happened at rock climbing. He also how told her that he'd got a perfect score in his spelling test at school, so it hadn't been a completely bad day.

When he saw the kitchen clock tick over to 7:20 p.m., Jack excused himself from dinner and headed for his room. As soon as he got there, he went over to his desk and signed on to the GPF secure website. On the home page was the latest news:

BREAKING STORY

A small passenger plane has gone missing over Mount Everest. It was carrying scientists and what is believed to be the first true Yeti skull ever recovered. If proven to be that of a Yeti, the skull will be the only verified evidence that the Abominable Snowman really existed, or might even exist still. Local rescue teams have been dispatched, but owing to high winds they are finding it hard to reach the mountain. A team of GPF agents trained in mountaineering will be sent to the region. All experts on Yeti folklore will also be called to the site.

After reading the article, Jack's eyes widened. He'd heard stories about the Abominable Snowman but he always thought they were made up. If what they were saying was true, there was a piece of valuable history lost on the mountain – not to mention the passengers on that plane.

As if on cue, Jack heard a gentle click and a whirring noise. According to his watch it was 7:30 p.m., and Whizzy, his trusty bedside globe, was starting to spin. Based on the information on the website, Jack had a pretty good idea where he was heading.

Jack was an agent with the Global Protection Force, or GPF, a special organization of junior agents dedicated to protecting 'that which cannot protect itself'. Since Jack had become a secret agent, he'd found and rescued countless stolen objects and people in trouble. Like the time he went to Kenya to capture some poachers who were killing elephants for their ivory.

Whizzy spun himself into a fury and popped a jigsaw piece out of his mouth. When Jack picked it up, he noticed it resembled a smile. He walked over to his Magic Map on the wall and looked at the continent of Asia. Sure enough, there was a spot under Tibet, in China, where the jigsaw piece could fit. He slotted it in and the name of the country showed up: 'NEPAL'.

It flashed once, then disappeared. Jack

raced over to his bed and pulled his Secret Agent Book Bag out from underneath. He tapped his Watch Phone for the code of the day, and when he received the word I-C-E, he entered it on the lock on his Book Bag.

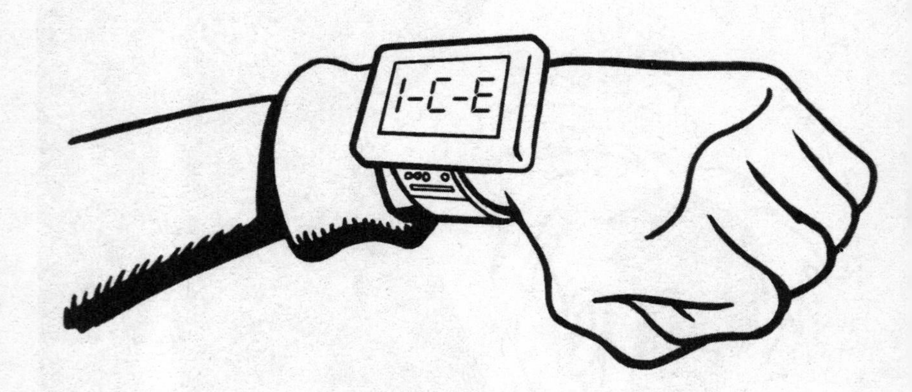

As soon as it popped open, Jack rifled through his bag, checking the contents. In there was his Polar Parka, his Flyboard, and his Handy Cuffs. The GPF had recently added some Crafty Crampons, flexible spikes that were attached to the bottom of your shoes to help them grip.

Quickly, Jack zipped up his Book Bag and stood in front of the Magic Map. As soon as the light inside Nepal grew bright enough to fill the room, Jack yelled, 'Off to Nepal!' Then the light flickered and burst, and swallowed him inside the Magic Map.

Chapter 3: Base Camp

Jack was surprised when he arrived, because Nepal wasn't at all what he was expecting. He wasn't standing in its capital city, Kathmandu, or on a snow-covered mountain or an icy cliff. Instead, he found himself on dry, rocky terrain, with lots of tents and empty oxygen canisters on the ground.

Jack recognized the spot right away. It was the 'Base Camp' of Everest in the Himalayas, where many famous mountain-climbing expeditions had started. It was where Sir Edmund Hillary and Sherpa Tenzing Norgay started their history-making ascent of Everest in 1953.

Jack was finding it difficult to breathe. Before climbing Everest, most mountain-climbers spent days, if not weeks, at Base Camp, getting used to the lack of oxygen in the air. There was a third less oxygen at the top of Mount Everest than there was at sea level: if someone was taken straight from sea level to the top, they'd die within minutes.

By acclimatizing at Base Camp, however, climbers were able to give their bodies the chance to make more red blood cells. More red blood cells meant that more oxygen could be taken in from the air. Because Jack hadn't had a chance to acclimatize yet, he was starting to feel dizzy.

He opened his Secret Agent Book Bag and pulled out his Oxygen Exchanger. In Australia, Jack had used the Oxygen Exchanger to breathe underwater. Here in the Himalayas, he could use it to create more red blood cells. It did this with the help of a red blood cell 'accelerator mist', which entered his mouth every time he breathed. As soon as he strapped on the Oxygen Exchanger, Jack started feeling better.

A voice came from beside him. 'Secret Agent Courage?'

Jack turned round. There, next to a canvas tent, stood a man. He was dressed in khaki-colored trousers and a long-sleeved

fleece with the GPF logo on it. He stuck out his hand towards Jack.

'Nice to meet you,' he said. 'I'm Alex Bell,' he added, 'leader of this GPF expedition.' Jack shook the man's hand. 'Where are the others?' he asked.

Almost as soon as Jack spoke, three other children materialized: two boys and a girl. When they realized how thin the air was, they too got out their Oxygen Exchangers. Mr Bell walked over to them and motioned for Jack to join him.

'Secret Agent Courage,' he said to Jack, 'these are Secret Agent Storm, Secret Agent Digger and Secret Agent Scarlet.'

He pointed to the children one by one.

Jack shook their hands. Secret Agent Storm looked older than him. He had striking blue eyes and strong-looking arms.

Secret Agent Digger was shorter than Storm. In fact, he was smaller than Jack. But he looked tough.

Scarlet, however, was slim and seemed shy. Jack tried not to frown as he wondered why on earth the GPF had called her in for the job.

'Right,' said Mr Bell. 'We'll need to work together on this one. No one climbs alone. The winds can be like a hurricane,' he explained. 'The crevasses are bottomless pits. The icefall is constantly moving. One mistake and you won't make it home for dinner tonight.'

Jack tried not to let anyone else see it, but he was more than a little nervous. After all, over the last century more than two hundred climbers had died trying to make it to the top of Everest. Jack looked at the other three. He wondered whether they realized how dangerous this mission would be.

Mr Bell pulled out a map. It was a detailed drawing of the route to the top of the mountain. An X marked the spot where they were standing.

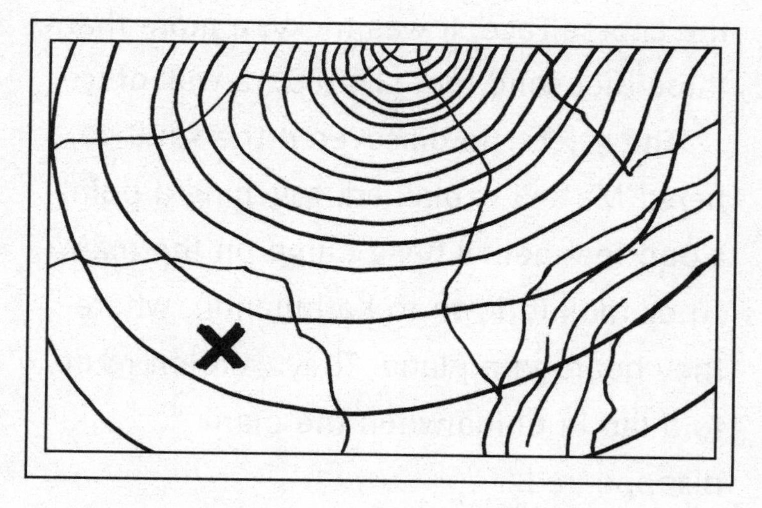

'This is us,' he said, pointing to where Base Camp was marked. 'A helicopter's going to fly you over the Khumbu Icefall and touch down on the Western Cwm.' (He pronounced it 'coom'.)

'Where's the missing plane?' asked Digger through his Oxygen Exchanger.

'Not sure,' said Mr Bell. 'We lost communication north of the icefall. They could be anywhere between there and the Lhotse Face.'

Jack hoped the plane wasn't north of the Lhotse Face. It was tricky; a more than three thousand foot climb up a wall of ice.

'The scientists discovered the skull here,' Mr Bell explained, touching a point 1,600 feet below Base Camp on the map. 'They took it down to Kathmandu, where they boarded a plane. They were en route to a lab in China when the plane disappeared.'

Jack looked at the other agents. They were listening carefully to Mr Bell.

'I need to stay here to wait for our Yeti experts,' the GPF man said. 'If any of you get into trouble, call me on your Watch Phone. And another thing – we've got company.'

'What do you mean?' asked Jack.

'We got word that another group is tracking the skull too,' he said. 'It could be the RSO.' The RSO, or Russian Secret Ops, was an international group of agents hired by shady Russian villains to do their dirty work.

'Why do they want the skull?' asked Storm.

'Who knows?' said Mr Bell. 'But assume they're armed with gadgets, and dangerous.'

Jack looked at Scarlet. Her eyes were closed. She looked like she was sleeping.

'What are you doing?' he asked her.

'Meditating,' she said.

Jack rolled his eyes at this weird girl. He turned to the boys. 'You ready?' he asked.

Storm, Digger and Jack stood up. Scarlet opened her eyes, and got up too. Mr Bell gave them each a firm handshake. 'Good luck,' he said. 'You're going to need it.'

Then Jack and the others headed towards the chopper.

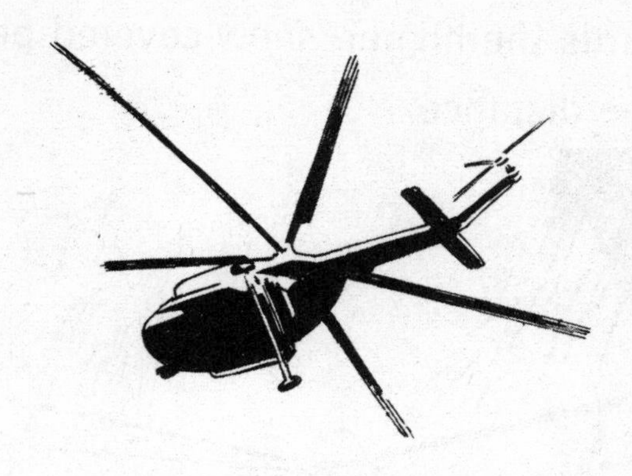

Chapter 4: The Expert

The GPF was working to develop a helicopter that could fly as high as the top of Everest. But until then, Jack and the others were stuck with the old ones they currently had on the mountain. This particular one looked like it had been around since the 1970s.

As the chopper's propeller started to whirl, the children climbed inside. Soon it lifted off. Dust blew up from the ground below them, and they moved swiftly towards the higher, snow-covered peaks in the distance.

Jack pulled his equipment out of his Book Bag. First he grabbed his Crafty Crampons. The GPF's Crafty Crampons were steel frames with twelve spikes that hooked onto the bottoms of your shoes. That way, you wouldn't slip on the ice. They became flexible if you needed to walk, or stayed rigid if you needed to do ice climbing. Jack strapped them onto his boots.

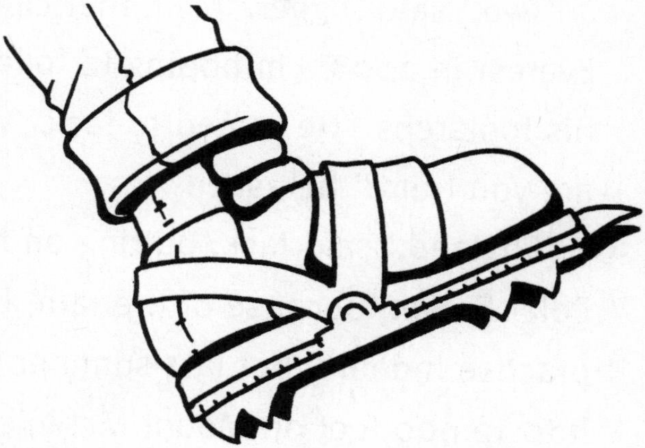

Next he checked his harness and ropes. They all seemed in good condition. He pulled out a drawstring bag and opened it. Inside was the GPF's Polar Parka. This kept you warm in extremely cold temperatures. Jack had used it in the Arctic before. Now it was going to be tested on Everest.

Digger turned to Storm. 'How long have you been climbing?' he asked, over the rattling hum of the helicopter.

'Three years,' said Storm. 'Most recently on Mount Rainier. You?'

'Two,' said Digger. 'My father climbed Everest in 2008. I'm hoping to follow in his footsteps.' He turned to Jack. 'Where are you from?' he asked.

'England,' said Jack, putting on his Polar Parka. 'Because of the rain, I mostly practise indoors, but last summer I made it to 12,000 feet on Mount McKinley.'

Digger and Storm looked impressed. Then the boys turned to Scarlet. Jack doubted she had much to say.

She rolled her eyes. 'If you must know,' she said, 'I've been climbing since I was little. In fact, I've just climbed Mount Kilimanjaro.'

The boys' mouths fell open. They

looked at Scarlet and her slight, fragile frame. There was no way she was telling the truth.

'I did it in seven days,' said Scarlet. 'A new record for someone my age.'

'Wait a minute,' said Digger. 'Is your real name Piper McKreeley? I think I read about you in the paper.'

'That's me,' said Secret Agent Scarlet matter-of-factly.

Jack was gobsmacked. Mount

Kilimanjaro was the highest mountain on the African continent. It was more than 19,000 feet above sea level. If Scarlet had indeed climbed it, she was more experienced than them. Jack made a mental note never to judge someone by their appearance again.

The helicopter jolted forward.

Jack looked out and saw that they were flying over the Khumbu Icefall, one of the most dangerous places on Everest. The icefall was like a frozen river that forced its way about three feet down the mountain every day. This meant that huge 'crevasses', or holes, could open up without warning. Large towers of ice called 'seracs' could fall on top of you.

As they passed over the icefall, Jack noticed, to the north, a smoother, flatter area covered in snow. This was the Western Cwm, their next destination.

Chapter 5:
The Valley of Silence

The helicopter lowered itself into the valley, and Jack and the others jumped out.

CRUNCH!

Their crampons dug into the icy snow. The sunlight bounced off the glacier, making it hard for them to see. The children put on their GPF Snow Shades to protect their eyes from snow blindness.

The helicopter pilot took off, leaving Jack, Storm, Digger and Scarlet behind.

Jack scanned his surroundings. Now he understood why mountaineers called the Western Cwm the 'Valley of Silence'. It was deathly quiet. There was no breeze, no birds, and no life. In the absence of wind, it was also blazing hot.

Jack looked at the temperature on his Watch Phone. It was 95°F. He shifted the temperature control setting on his Polar Parka from 'warm' to 'cool'. It certainly wasn't what he was expecting on Everest.

Flicking a switch on the side of his Snow Shades, Jack tried to locate the plane. Like the Google Goggles, the GPF Snow Shades had a zooming feature. Except for a crevasse followed by an ice boulder, there was nothing in sight.

'I wonder where it is,' said Jack. 'Planes don't just disappear.'

'They do if someone wants them to,' said Scarlet.

‘Do you think it was planned?’ asked Storm.

‘Maybe,’ said Scarlet. ‘After all, they were carrying precious cargo. If the Russians are after it, maybe they’re the ones who brought it down.’

Jack hadn’t thought of that before. He’d assumed that the plane had accidentally crashed. If someone wanted to get their hands on the skull, this was the perfect way to do it. Make the plane disappear, and take off with the cargo when nobody was watching.

'Do you think it's real?' asked Digger.

'The Yeti?' said Storm, shrugging his shoulders. 'People have taken photos of weird footprints. Others swear to having seen an ape-like creature as high as 19,000 feet.'

Jack stared into the distance. They were about that altitude now. He wondered whether there was a Yeti lurking somewhere on the mountain, watching them.

Not wasting any time, Scarlet grabbed a small H-shaped frame from her Book Bag and began to lengthen the ends. After a minute she'd created a sturdy aluminium ladder.

'The plane's probably on the other side of this crevasse,' she said, pointing to the huge crack in the ice ahead.

Scarlet walked up to the edge of the hole and lowered the ladder over the crevasse. Now it was touching the other side of the chasm. Fastening the ends of the ladder to the ground with ice stakes, Scarlet tied a rope to the first rung.

'Let's go for it,' she said.

Scarlet went first. With steady legs, she stepped on each rung, careful not to fall or drop the rope. When she got to the other side, she tied the rope to the top of the ladder, and used two more ice stakes to fasten it to the ice. Thanks to Scarlet, the others had a makeshift handrail they could hold onto when they crossed the bridge.

Next it was Jack's turn. He put his foot on the ladder.

CLINK.

The crampons made a loud noise against the rung. He took another step.

CLINK.

Jack was really sweating now, not only because it was hot, but also because of what was below: a huge vertical drop between two gigantic slabs of ice. As he looked down, he noticed that the color of the ice changed from white at the top to dark blue at the bottom. As wacky as it sounded, Jack thought this crevasse was

one of the most beautiful he'd ever seen.

Jack had been over several crevasses before. In fact, when he visited Mount McKinley in America, he'd learned how to rescue people who'd fallen down one. Recently, a climber in Europe had died when he fell down a crevasse and his partner was unable to save him.

Carefully, Jack continued to walk along the ladder until he reached the other side.

Storm was next. He made it across without a problem. The only one left was Digger. As soon as he put his foot out, however, Jack knew that something was wrong. Digger's leg was shaking with nerves.

'It'll be all right, Digger!' shouted Jack.

But when the boy tried to step on the second rung, he slipped. His safety rope was pulled off his harness.

'AHHHH!'

His body sailed down the crevasse. Jack and the others raced to the edge. They shouted down to him, but Digger didn't answer. They shook their heads. What Mr Bell had said was true: Digger wouldn't be going home for dinner tonight.

Just then, Jack spotted something. He flicked his Snow Shades to zoom in again, and spied a small ice shelf about fifty feet down. Unbelievably, there was something lying motionless on it. It was Digger!

‘I’ll get him,’ said Jack. ‘Just be ready to pull us up,’ he told the others.

Quickly, he pulled his Klimbing Kit out of his bag. This was a circular case with a series of long nylon ropes. He tied a spike to the end of one and, at the push of a button, shot it down the crevasse. The spike torpedoed into the ice above Digger and fixed itself there.

After tying another spike to the other end of the rope, Jack shot that one into the ice boulder behind him. Tugging on the cord to make sure it was secure, he turned to Storm and Scarlet.

‘Wish me luck,’ he said.

He then threw a shorter rope over the cord and zip-lined into the crevasse.

Chapter 6: The Crevasse

Because of the steep slope, Jack was moving fast. He braced himself before he smashed into the wall above Digger. Shaking off the pain, he jumped down next to the boy: he had to hurry. He didn't know how long the shelf would hold the weight of two people.

'Digger,' said Jack, shaking him gently. 'Are you OK?'

Digger grimaced as Jack touched his arm, but at least he was alive. Jack

opened his bottle of pungent GPF Smelling Salts and rubbed it underneath Digger's nose. That seemed to wake him up, but he was still groggy.

'You're pretty lucky,' said Jack. 'Any further over and we wouldn't be having this conversation.'

He unhooked the spike from the ice and tied the rope to their harnesses. When he was ready, Jack yanked on it. Soon, there was another tug from above. It was Storm and Scarlet pulling them up. It took about ten minutes, but soon Jack and Digger had made it to safety.

'I think his arm is broken,' said Jack.

Although the GPF's Fix-It Tape could heal cuts and minor wounds, it couldn't repair bone. 'He's in a pretty bad way,' he added. 'One of us needs to get him back to Base Camp.'

Scarlet offered herself. 'I'll stay and radio for the helicopter.'

Jack remembered the helicopter pilot saying something about making a food drop at a neighboring village.

'It could take hours for you to get back,' he said. 'We'll have to go on without you.'

'That's OK,' said Scarlet with a smile. 'I'll catch up.'

Seeing as Scarlet had climbed Kilimanjaro in a record time, Jack and Storm decided to agree to her plan. The boys waited until Scarlet had helped Digger back over the ladder, then they set off towards the boulder ahead – and, hopefully, the missing plane.

Chapter 7: The Pilot's Help

It took them thirty minutes, but Jack and Storm managed to climb the vertical mass of ice blocking their way. As soon as they were on the other side, they switched their Snow Shades back to 'zoom'. This time they could see something in the near distance. It was the missing plane!

The propellers were gently turning round. Underneath the plane were metal squares that linked together to form a runway. From what Jack could tell, it didn't look like the plane had crashed. In fact, it looked like someone had intentionally landed it on the Western Cwm.

But where were the crew and passengers?

Except for the plane, there didn't seem to be anything or anybody in sight. Jack and Storm switched on their boots' Mine Alert feature. Instantly, a green line shot out of the tips, scanning the ground for booby-traps like bombs.

Slowly they walked around to the main door of the plane, which was hanging open. Jack peered inside. There, tied up with tape on their mouths, lay two men. Jack reckoned they must be the missing scientists.

Storm rushed over to one of them and pulled the tape off his mouth. The man's eyes looked glazed and his head slumped down. It was clear he was suffering from altitude sickness.

Jack and Storm each pulled a spare Oxygen Exchanger out of their Book Bag. They strapped them onto the men. After a few moments one of the scientists mumbled something.

'Mero nam Roshan,' he said slowly. He was barely able to string his words together. 'Malai topaiko.'

Jack pulled out his Secret Language Decoder. As the man spoke, it told Jack what he was saying in English.

'They took the skull,' the man said, gasping for air. 'They left us to die.'

Storm took his Language Decoder out too. He switched it to 'Nepalese'. It translated what he was saying into the men's native language.

'Who left you?' asked Storm.

'The pilot,' said the man. 'When he landed, he opened a door. Another man and a boy appeared.'

'A boy?' asked Jack, confused.

The scientist nodded. 'The three of them tied us up.'

Jack was surprised. He didn't realize the RSO had junior agents. As far as he knew, the GPF was the only organization that relied on the skills and intelligence of children.

'Did they tell you their names?' asked Jack. 'Did they say where they were going?'

The man shook his head. 'Only that their client was waiting for the skull. But it hasn't been long since they left.'

The fact that they'd only just departed gave Jack hope. This meant that, with any luck, he and Storm could quickly track the villains and get the skull back. But they had to take care of the scientists first.

Even though they now had oxygen, the men needed to get down the mountain.

It was the only way to cure their sickness. Since they weren't climbers, they needed the help of an expert.

Jack called Mr Bell on his Watch Phone. They agreed that Storm would escort the men down and meet Scarlet at Base Camp. From there, Scarlet and Storm would start all over again and make their way back up to Jack.

In the meantime, Jack was to search for clues. If possible, he was to find the villains' escape route. Now Jack was going to go it alone against the bad guys, and against the unwelcome terrain of one of the deadliest mountains on Earth.

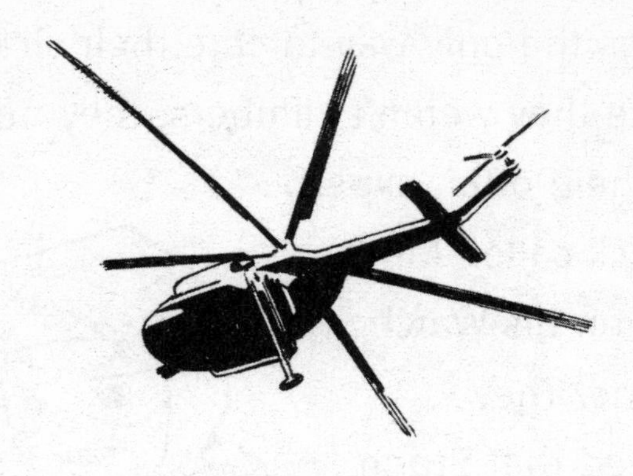

Chapter 8: The Annoying Surprise

After Storm and the men had left, Jack surveyed the snow around the plane. As he expected, there were fresh tracks. The boot prints headed north towards the Lhotse Face – the vertical wall of ice in the distance. This could mean only one thing: the thieves were heading over the mountain.

On the other side was Tibet, in China. From there, several routes led back to Russia. There was the Trans-Siberian

Railway, the longest railway in the world, which linked China to Russia. There were also a number of smaller airports, any of which the villains could use.

Jack reported back to Mr Bell, who alerted the Tibetan authorities. But the base of Mount Everest was huge, and there was no way they or the GPF could surround the entire mountain. Jack's only choice was to set off after them on foot.

He zoomed his Snow Shades across the Western Cwm and up to Camp II. Camp II was halfway between where Jack was standing and the Lhotse Face. There, in the distance, he spied three figures. Since they were dressed in white, he nearly missed them. But he was sure these must be the thieves.

For a few moments Jack watched them move. The two taller ones walked quickly, but the small one, possibly the boy, was

slower. If the boy was tiring, there was a chance that Jack might catch up with them. He started to make his way after them.

The higher in altitude he went, the colder it got and the longer it took. Jack switched his Polar Parka back to 'warm'. Even with the help of his Oxygen Exchanger, he was feeling tired – more tired than he'd ever felt in his life. For every step he took, he had to wait at least a minute before he could take another one.

Several hours passed, and Jack finally made it to the Lhotse Face – higher in altitude than he'd ever been before. For a moment he thought how proud his parents would be, and how impressed his missing brother, Max, would be with him too. Despite Max's courage, he had never really got into mountain climbing. But Jack had always liked heights. As Jack stood at the base of the Lhotse Face, he stared at the three figures above him. They had no idea that he was only about 150 feet below them. He carefully thought through his options.

He could catch them with the GPF's Tornado, which could send a speeding rope to capture all three at the same time. Or he could use the Spray Gun to send a vial of sleeping potion their way. But there were only two vials in his bag – not enough to knock them all out. Lastly, there was the Net Tosser, but gravity was against him. There was no way he could throw it upwards without it falling straight back down.

Jack decided to use his Tornado. That way he could disable all three bad guys at once. He lifted the Tornado out of his Book Bag and

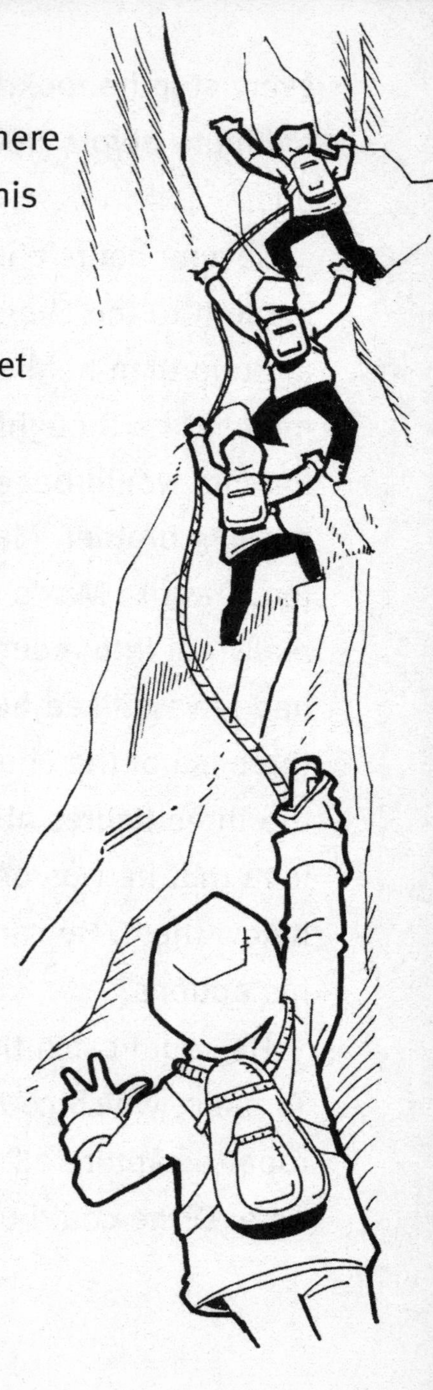

programmed it to seek the crooks. With a push of a button, three ropes spiralled out. But because it was so cold, they froze in mid-air.

They fell to the ground like steel rods, making a clink as they crashed. Not only could Jack hear the noise: so too could the climbers. They had spotted him. One of them pulled something out of his bag and threw it down. Before Jack could react, a huge net opened over him. It fastened itself to the ground, trapping him inside. Jack pulled at the sides, but it

was impossible to get out. From above, a high-pitched boy's voice rang out.

'Better luck next time, Stalwart!' it said.

Stunned that someone actually knew his name, Jack looked up. The boy pulled down his mask to expose his face. It was none other than Marko Mayer, Jack's rival from the indoor rock-climbing center.

Chapter 9:
The Split

Jack's head started to spin. How and why was Marko Mayer on Everest? Maybe there was some funny gas in the net that was causing him to hallucinate. Or maybe he was suffering from altitude sickness. But the fact that he felt fine told him that his brain wasn't going soft. Did this mean that Marko was an agent like Jack, but for the bad guys?

'I told you I was a better climber than you!' Marko shouted down to Jack. The man beside Marko said something to him. He seemed to be telling Marko to focus on what he was doing.

'You're nothing but a has-been!' Marko went on. 'You used to be a better climber than me, but now look at me! I've nearly reached the top of the world!'

The other man was motioning for the boy to be quiet.

Marko ignored him. 'The last thing you're going to see of me,' he yelled, 'is my butt as I climb over to the other side.'

At that comment, Jack felt furious. He didn't know how and when Marko had joined the Russians. Frankly, he had no idea why they'd chosen such an annoying boy. All Jack wanted to do was rip him off the ice and wipe that silly grin off his face.

Just then, he heard a noise. It was coming from above. The ice above Marko

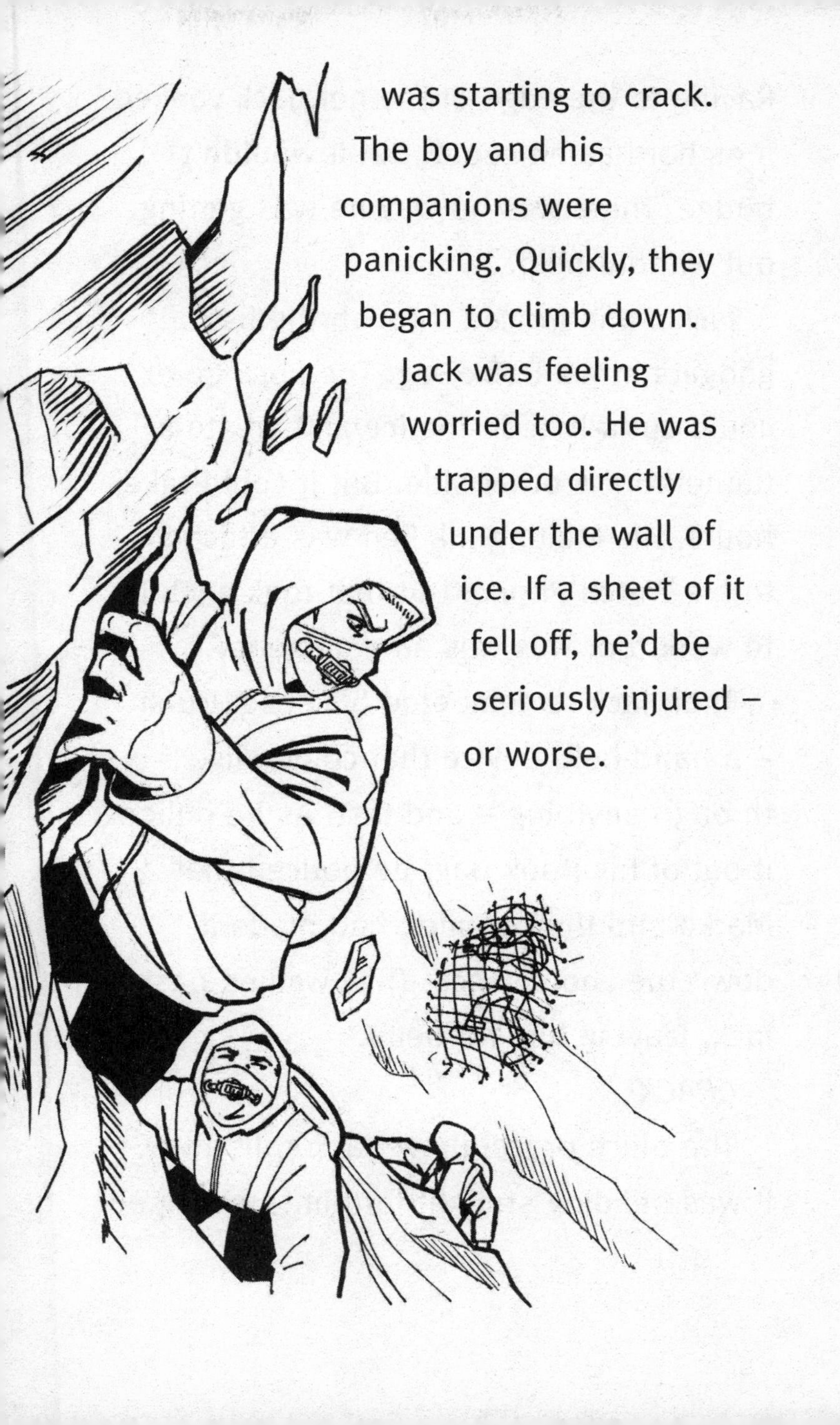

was starting to crack. The boy and his companions were panicking. Quickly, they began to climb down. Jack was feeling worried too. He was trapped directly under the wall of ice. If a sheet of it fell off, he'd be seriously injured – or worse.

Racing to the edge of the net, Jack yanked it as hard as he could. But it wouldn't budge. There was no way he was getting out without help.

Jack's mind raced through the list of gadgets in his Book Bag. The Rock Corer could cut a hole in the ice and create a tunnel to the other side. But it could take hours. His Melting Ink Pen was attached to his Watch Phone. But that took a while to work too. This was an emergency.

Then Jack remembered his Laser Burst – a hand-held device that could slice through anything – and fast. As he pulled it out of his Book Bag, he noticed that Marko and the two men had made it down the Lhotse Face. They walked past Jack, leaving him for dead.

CRACK!

The piece of ice above Jack split away. It was heading straight for him! He swiped his Laser Burst through the net and dived through the hole just as the giant slab crashed to the ground where he'd been standing.

KABOOM!

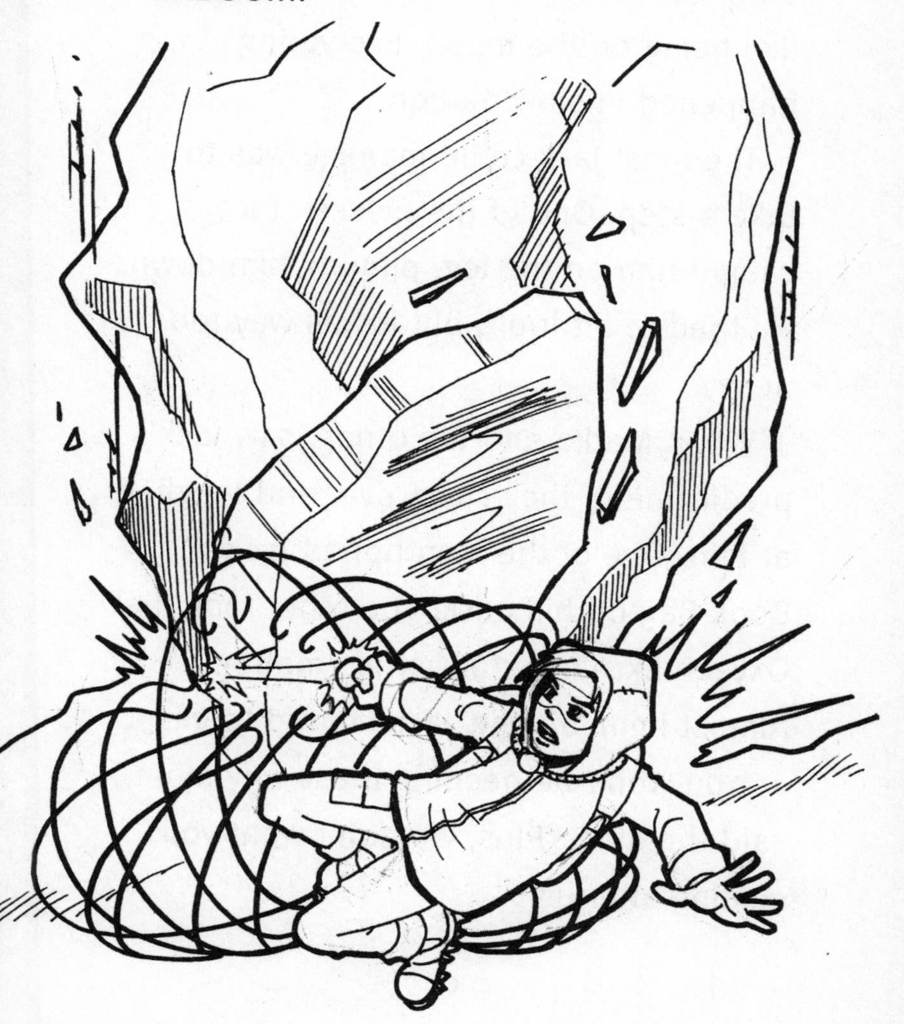

The ground shook.

The massive chunk of ice split into pieces that tumbled towards Jack. He tried to get up and run, but there was no such thing as running on Mount Everest. It was like being on the moon. Everything happened in slow motion.

The most Jack could manage was to take a step. One of the pieces of ice caught him on the leg, pinning him down. He tried to lift it off, but it was way too heavy.

When Marko and the others saw Jack's predicament, they came over and laughed at him. One of the men ripped Jack's Book Bag off his back. The other took the Oxygen Exchanger out of his mouth. Almost immediately, Jack started to gasp.

'You won't be needing these any more,' said the man. 'Plus, we don't want you coming after us.'

Marko and his companions turned and headed towards the Western Cwm. They were going to escape by way of the southern route now. Maybe, Jack thought, they'd changed their minds after seeing that falling ice on the Lhotse Face.

The man who'd taken Jack's Book Bag tossed it into the snow. The other one threw away his Oxygen Exchanger. Jack figured it was to lighten their load.

Jack was really struggling now. Without oxygen, his brain was turning fuzzy. His body hadn't had a chance to get used to the height, because the Oxygen Exchanger had done it for him. Desperately, he looked around for something – anything – that could set him free. He spotted his Laser Burst poking out of the snow. He had dropped it when he jumped through the net, and now it was out of reach.

However, there was a powerful magnet

on Jack's Watch Phone. He tapped a few buttons and activated the Magnetic Pull. As he placed his wrist on the snow, it started to vibrate. The Laser Burst flew towards his wrist and stuck to the face of the Watch Phone.

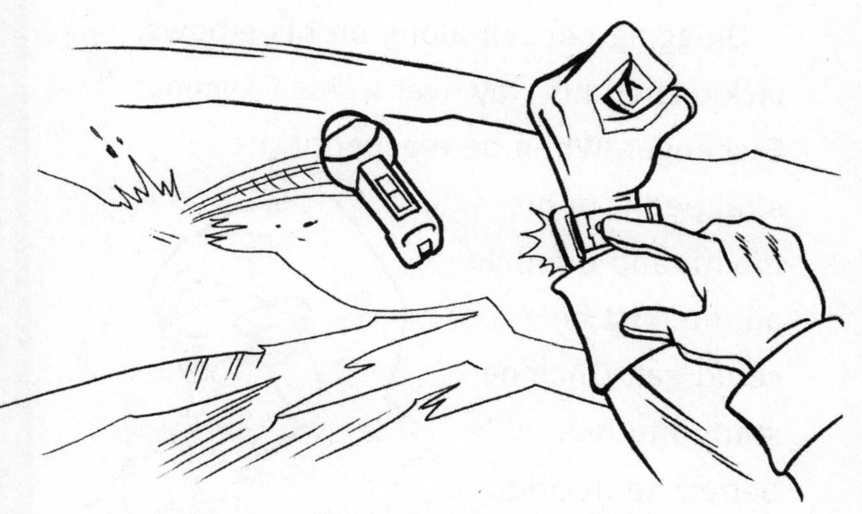

Grabbing the gadget with his other hand, Jack sent a powerful beam from the Laser Burst towards the ice. The heat from the laser started to melt it. It took a while, but eventually Jack was able to set himself free.

Relieved, he stood up, but soon collapsed to the ground. His body was disoriented; it was starting to malfunction. He saw that his Oxygen Exchanger lay not too far away. If Jack could get to it, it would save his life.

Dragging himself along on his elbows, Jack inched his way over to his Oxygen Exchanger. When he reached it, he strapped it to his mouth and drank in all the mist he could get. Once he started to feel better, he decided it was time to follow Marko and the others.

Jack used his Snow Shades to zero in on the crooks. By now, they were nearing the lower portion of the Western Cwm. As far as they knew, Jack was the only agent after them. And they thought he was trapped at the Lhotse Face.

Jack called Mr Bell, who patched him through to Scarlet and Storm. They were about to cross the ladder over the crevasse at the foot of the Western Cwm. Jack told them to hold off and wait. He had a plan to catch the crooks. If all went as he hoped, then Jack could finally nab Marko and show him who was boss.

Chapter 10: The Power of Light

Scarlet and Storm were waiting there patiently when they saw three figures making their way over the boulder in front of the crevasse. As the figures touched down, they spied Scarlet and Storm on the other side.

'Where do you think you're going?' Scarlet yelled.

A high-pitched voice rang out. 'Get out of our way!' shouted the boy.

A calm male voice added, 'Move – or I

will have to terminate you.'

'We can't let you pass,' said Scarlet. 'That skull belongs in a museum, not in the hands of—'

ZAP!

Before she could finish, a blast of light zapped her in the stomach. It threw her backwards and she skidded along in the snow. She groaned in pain.

Shocked, Storm looked at the man's hand. It held a long tube with smoke coming out of the end. He'd never seen one of those before, but he knew that the Russians had the power to harness light and use it as a weapon. Secret Agent Courage had written about it in a GPF memo when he returned from his mission in Russia.

'I'll give you one more chance,' growled the man. 'Let us pass, or you'll suffer the same fate.' The boy standing beside him started to snigger.

Storm knew there was only one gadget that could make this guy drop his weapon. But it was in his Book Bag. If he could only reach for it—

ZAP!

A bolt of light hit Storm too, sending him spinning into the air and knocking him out.

Marko started cackling. 'You showed them!' he said. 'Way to go!'

'Settle down,' said the man. 'A bit of self-control will serve you well in this job.'

Another voice came from behind Marko: 'I'll say,' it said.

Marko and the two men whipped round. Standing above them on the top of the boulder was none other than Jack. Quickly, he lifted his Lava Laser and fired it at the Russian's weapon. The GPF's

Lava Laser made the metal so hot that it burned the man's hand.

'YOOOWWW!'

The man instantly dropped the weapon and plunged his hands into the snow to cool them down. Shocked, Marko didn't know what to do. Jack took out his Net Tosser and threw it out over the crooks. The net covered the two adults, but Marko had managed to avoid it.

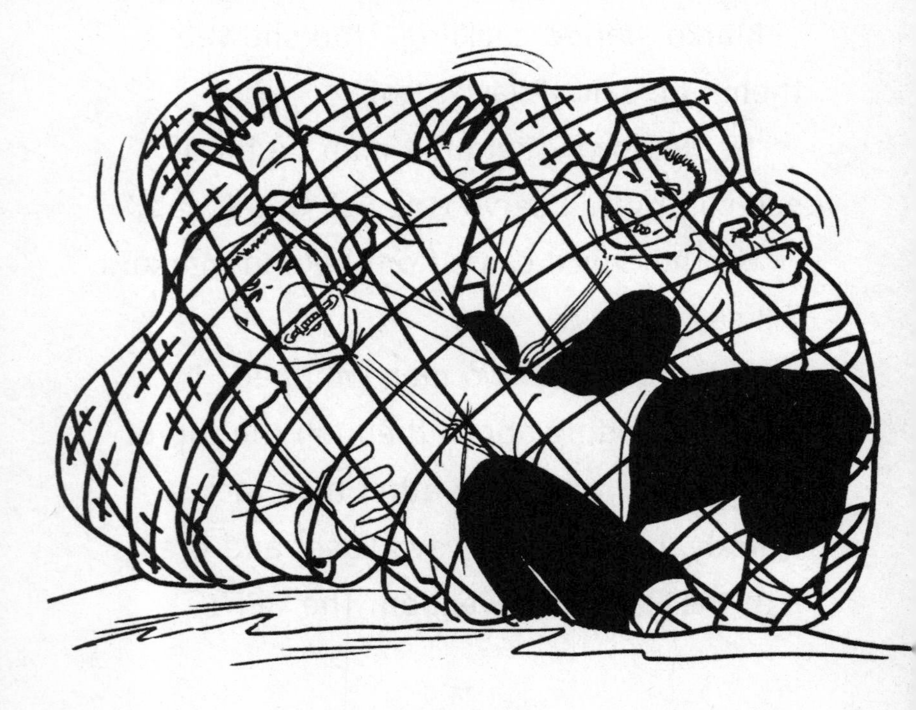

Jack abseiled down the boulder and unhooked himself from the safety rope. He went as quickly as he could, but Marko had already crossed the crevasse using the ladder. Holding his hands up, Marko showed the ice stakes that had once secured the ladder to the ground. With a push, he shoved the ladder down into the crevasse. It pinged off the walls and fell into the void.

Separating the boys was now a thirty-foot-wide hole in the ice.

'Let's see you get across that,' said Marko. 'You can arrest us,' he screamed, 'but you'll never get the skull!'

Just then, Jack heard the noise of an approaching helicopter. He breathed a sigh of relief. Reinforcements were arriving, and not a moment too soon.

Hanging from the belly of the chopper was a basket tied to a rope. When Marko

opened his backpack and took out something wrapped in cloth, Jack suddenly realized that this was no rescue – this was the 'pick-up': the mastermind behind the theft was collecting his prize.

Now Jack had to stop Marko and bring down a chopper.

But he couldn't do it until he'd crossed the crevasse. He didn't have a ladder like Scarlet and there wasn't enough slope for his Klimbing Kit. It was risky, but Jack had no choice but to use a gadget that had never been tested on mountains. It was the GPF's Flyboard, and it lay in his Book Bag.

Chapter 11: The Risky Crossing

The GPF's Flyboard was like a skateboard, with two small hydrogen-powered engines at the back. It could skate on ice, roll on tarmac or fly over land at a speed of twenty-five miles an hour. Here on Everest, however, Jack wasn't sure whether it would work at all.

After snapping his Flyboard together, Jack stepped onto it. As soon as he did so, he tested the 'air' feature. The Flyboard struggled and coughed. It

managed to raise itself two feet off the ground. Usually it flew at three times that height. However, Jack was so desperate, he decided to take the risk.

Pulling his Klimbing Kit out of his bag, he quickly tied the end of a rope to a spike and shot it into the upper wall of the crevasse. He then tied the other end of the rope to his harness.

Jack and the Flyboard travelled slowly over the empty void. But as soon as he reached the middle, the machine's

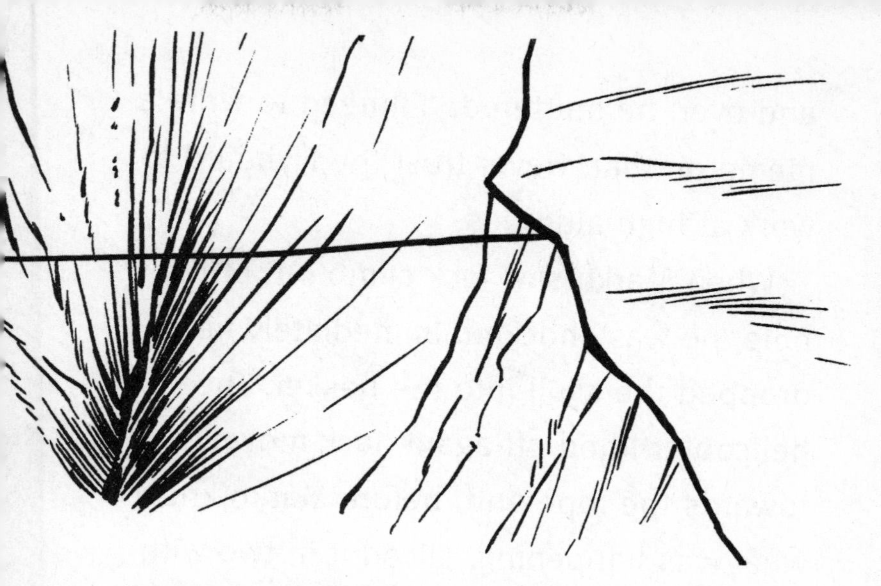

hydrogen engines spluttered to a stop. Instantly, Jack and the Flyboard tumbled down into the hole.

'AHHH!'

As he fell, Jack felt as if he was in some sort of icy cold dream. Then his body was jolted to a stop. He looked up at the spike on the side of the wall that had stopped him from falling any further. He secretly thanked the GPF for it, and climbed the rope until he reached the lip of the crevasse. As he pulled himself up and over, he muttered, ‘I’ll need to write a memo on that: Never trust the Flyboard to work at high altitudes.’

When Marko saw Jack climb out of the hole, he was shocked. Immediately he dropped the skull into the basket. The helicopter lifted off again. Jack moved towards the rope and, before Marko knew what was happening, sliced it in two with his Laser Burst. The basket and its contents dropped at least ten feet before crash-landing in the soft snow.

‘Hey!’ yelled Marko. ‘What are you doing?’

A man’s face popped out through the open door of the chopper. He scowled at Jack and yelled at him in Russian, threatening him with his shaking fist.

‘I’m doing what you should have done,’ said Jack, putting the package in his Book Bag. ‘I’m returning the skull to the scientists.’

'But scientists don't pay you a million dollars!' said Marko. He pointed to the man angrily hanging out of the helicopter. 'Give it to him,' he went on, 'and you and I can split the money.'

'No way,' said Jack.

Seeing that Jack wasn't about to switch sides, Marko made a run for it. He jumped for the severed rope, but unless the pilot lowered the chopper, there was no way he was going to reach it. The man issued one last threat, then the helicopter started to fly off.

'Hey!' Marko shouted. 'Where are you going?'

'You should never trust a crook,' Jack told him.

Tapping a few commands into his Watch Phone, Jack initiated the GPF Scrambling Device. The device could interfere with the controls of airplanes and helicopters so that they were unable to fly properly. Before Jack and Marko knew it, the crippled helicopter was on its way back down to the Western Cwm.

As soon as it landed, Jack climbed inside and placed the GPF's Handy Cuffs on the man and his pilot. The cuffs were strips of pliable plastic that hardened tight when the ends were joined.

When Jack got a better look at the mastermind, he realized it was none other than Alik Fedorov, the famous collector of bizarre pieces of history. His collection included a 600-million-year-old dinosaur egg, and teeth from one of the first cavemen. Jack had no doubt that he was after the skull because he wanted to add it to his collection.

Jack left the helicopter to search for Marko. He found him walking in circles and talking to himself, looking very worried.

'What should I do?' he was saying. 'Where should I go?'

Jack grabbed his wrists and wrapped a Handy Cuff around them too.

'I know just the place,' he said with a smile.

Jack knew that the punishment for stealing was jail time. Or, in the case of a child, a visit to the juvenile detention center.

Marko slumped down into the snow. 'I heard that my real father was a Russian spy,' he muttered, 'and I wanted to be just like him.'

Jack sympathized with him. After all, he'd joined the GPF so that he could find out more about his brother, Max. But Jack and Marko were different. Jack didn't turn to crime. Instead, he'd joined an organization that fought for good.

Once he had the thieves under control, Jack hurried over to Scarlet and Storm. They'd definitely been hit with something powerful. Jack bent down and put some Smelling Salts under their noses.

Instantly, they started to wake up.

When they came to, they were surprised to see Marko, a helicopter and a net full of men – all captured singlehandedly by none other than Secret Agent Courage.

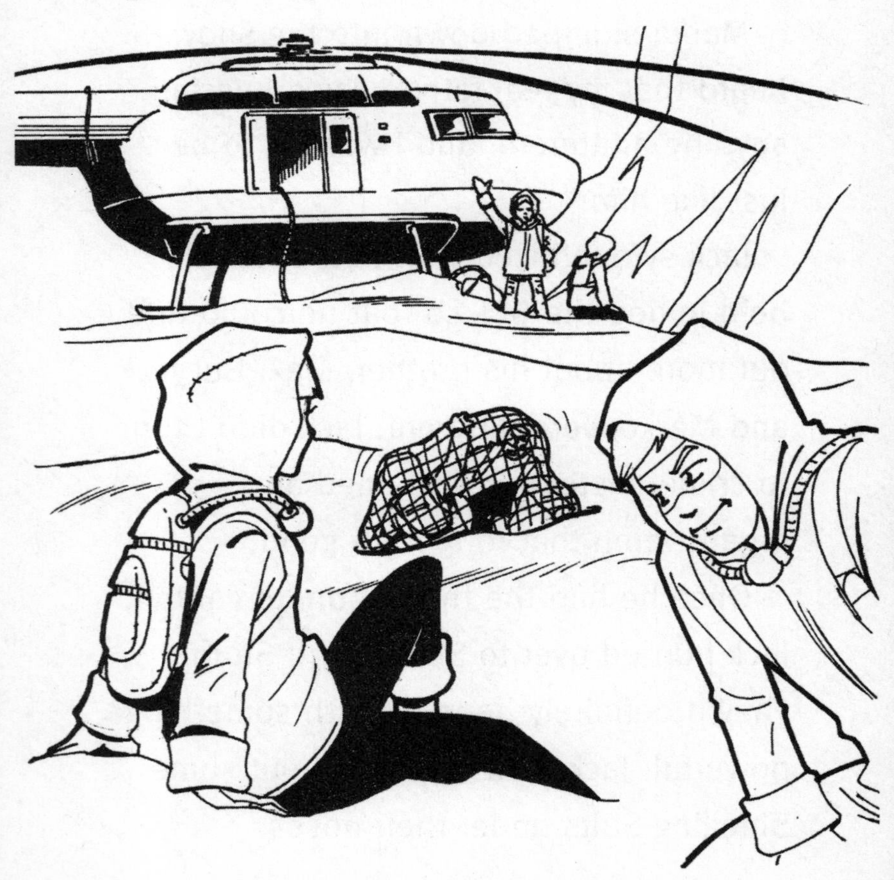

'Nice work,' said Storm.

Jack smiled. 'Thanks,' he said. 'But I couldn't have done it without you.'

The three agents radioed down to Mr Bell, who sent out a rescue helicopter. This time it was full of Nepalese police, come to take the thieves away. Jack released the Net Tosser and the police descended on the adults, dragging them along by their ears. Then they pulled a squealing Marko up off the snow.

As the police took Marko to the helicopter, Jack leaned over to him. 'What was that about being on top of the world?' he said.

Marko sneered at Jack, then looked away.

Chapter 12: The City of Temples

When Jack, Scarlet and Storm got back down to Base Camp, Mr Bell, Digger, the scientists and the Yeti experts were all waiting for them. Jack handed the wrapped skull to the scientist he'd first spoken to on the plane. 'This is for you,' he said.

The man's eyes danced with happiness. He quickly unwrapped the skull. When the Yeti experts saw it, they gasped.

'This is unbelievable!' said one. 'We've

never seen anything like it.'

Staring at everyone was an enormous white skull with large eye sockets and some teeth still in its jawbone. The top of the skull had a large ridge along it.

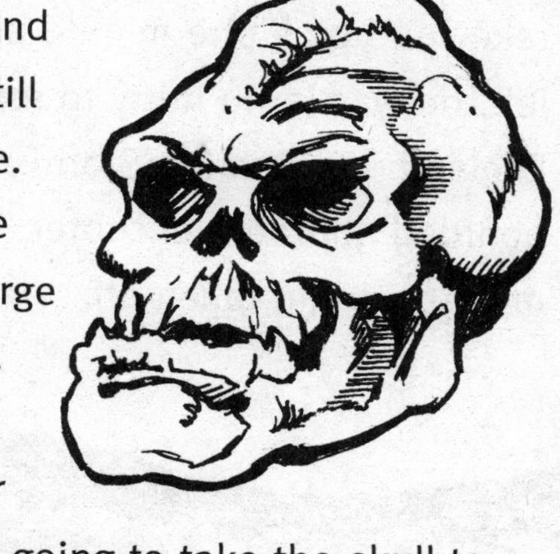

Mr Bell studied it. 'Mr Rohan here is going to take the skull to the lab in China, where it was originally headed,' he explained. 'There they can test its authenticity. This time we're going to arrange armed transport.'

Mr Bell showed the scientists and the Yeti experts to a guarded truck, then returned to Jack and the others. He congratulated them on a 'job well done'. As a treat, he offered to take them to the capital city, Kathmandu.

Jack had never been to Kathmandu before, and since the Magic Map could take you home one minute after you'd left, he was in no hurry to return to England. He, Scarlet, Storm and Digger boarded another helicopter. Within minutes it had taken off.

As they went down the mountain, things grew a lot less scrubby and became more lush. Jack saw green rice terraces, white rapids and rivers, and houses stacked on the hillside. Then he spotted ancient red and brown temples. The valleys around Kathmandu were very different from the place where Jack had grown up. He thought

they were really beautiful.

After a journey of two hours the team landed and transferred to a car. As they drove into the city of Kathmandu, Jack was surprised by how busy and colorful it was. There were shops selling everything from robes and scarves to cameras and rugs.

Ahead was Durbar Square, the site of no less than twelve ancient temples. Mr Bell opened the car door, and Jack, Storm, Scarlet and Digger jumped out. Wandering over to one of the temples, Jack spun one of the prayer wheels and thanked the gods for their help. He also asked for the safe return of his brother, Max.

Heading into the streets, they soon found a local restaurant. They ate traditional dumplings and tried a local meat curry. It was spicy, but Jack really

loved it. They chased the food down with some chiya (the local spiced tea), and toasted the success of their mission.

After finishing their meal, they said goodbye to Mr Bell and each other. One by one, they disappeared into the streets of Kathmandu. After all, they needed to get home.

Storm lost himself in a temple. Digger blended into the café on the corner. Scarlet hid herself amongst the scarves in the market. Jack found himself in front of a local school. He pulled some pencils out of his trouser pocket and gave them to the children who were milling around, looking at him hopefully. Walking down the side alley, he found what he was looking for – the perfect spot to vanish without being noticed.

Pulling his Portable Map out of his Book Bag, Jack laid it on the ground. The map was like the one on his wall at home, only it was compact enough to fit in his Book Bag. Pulling out a tiny flag of England, Jack stuck it on top of that country.

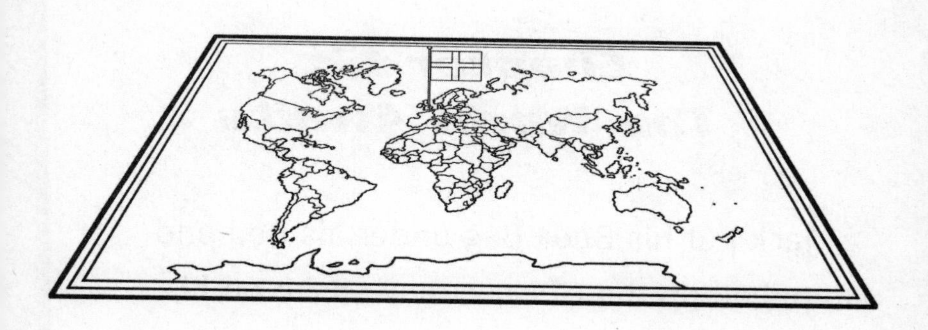

When a small light appeared, he said, 'Off to England!' There was a burst of light which swallowed up Jack and the map. The next thing Jack knew, he was in his room at home.

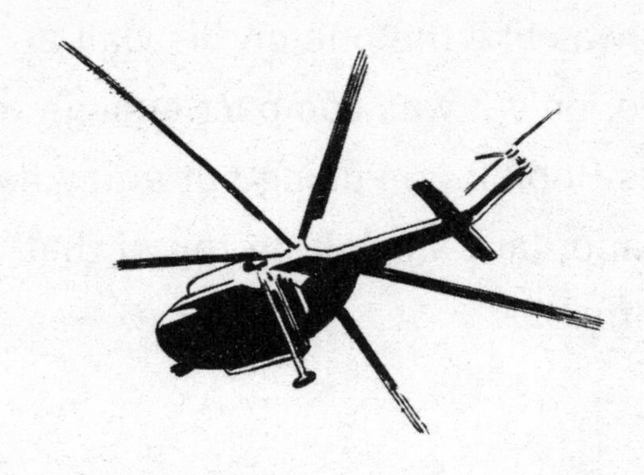

Chapter 13: The World Awaits

Jack put his Book Bag under his bed and pulled up the GPF secure website on his computer. A news bulletin had recently been posted.

BREAKING STORY

The thieves who attempted to steal a possible Yeti skull from Nepal have been captured by a team of GPF agents. Secret Agents Courage, Scarlet, Storm and Digger successfully apprehended members of the RSO (Russian Secret Ops), who were acting on behalf of notorious collector, Alik Fedorov.

The RSO hijacked a plane, stole the skull and left its scientists at high altitude on Mount Everest. Thanks to the bravery and mountaineering skills of Courage, Scarlet, Storm and Digger, not only were the scientists saved, but the skull was returned to the men who found it.

The skull is now en route to a lab in China, where it will be tested for authenticity. The whole world awaits confirmation as to whether it belongs to a real Abominable Snowman. By this time next week we will know for sure.

The three RSO agents, including one boy, are currently being held by the police in Kathmandu. From there, they will be returned to their native countries to face possible conviction and jail time.

Jack smiled as he logged off the computer. He didn't have to worry about Marko bugging him at the climbing center any more.

He changed into his pajamas, brushed his teeth and pulled out his book on mountaineering. Crawling under the covers, he opened it to the first page. Staring at him were Sir Edmund Hillary and Sherpa Tenzing Norgay on the day they climbed Everest in 1953.

While Jack hadn't actually made it to the top, he'd come close. He was probably the youngest person ever to reach the base of the Lhotse Face. Guinness World Records wasn't there to record his triumph, but what he'd done was nothing less than remarkable. Climbing more than 26,000 feet was a massive feat for anyone, let alone a child.

Jack wondered whether Hillary and Norgay were looking on him with pride. Pleased by his success in getting rid of the bad guys yet again, Jack closed the book and wondered what sort of challenge he'd be thrown next. Whatever it was, he told himself, he'd be more than ready.

Look out for Jack's final mission

— coming in October 2011

SECRET AGENT NOTES

SECRET AGENT NOTES

SECRET AGENT NOTES